THE SAGA OF

SEASON ONE

:#EMM

:file :GRUDGE/SIGN :07232017 :0918
:chatter :EVIL MONKEY MAN
:contact season :ONE of THREE

:transmission details
:story :N BLAKE SEALS
:art :BUTCH MAPA
:color and letters :Blake
:cover :Butch Mapa with color by K Michael Russell
:edits :Vincent Ferrante
:logos and design :Blake

:inspired by "Evil Monkey Man" as performed by FL!NG Lo!S
:composed by Frank Anthony Roseto
:character design :Blake with Russ Braun

:©2020 Nicholas Blake Seals & Frank Anthony Roseto
:dba EMM Holdings, Inc.
:all rights reserved

:outcome :CLASSIFIED SECRET :end :###
:a monarch comics presentation

THE SAGA OF EVIL MONKEY MAN! Season One. ISBN 978-1-7358368-2-9 Published by Monarch Comics, LLC.
Evil Monkey Man, including all related concepts, characters, logos, and images are © and TM 2020 by Nicholas Blake Seals
and Frank Anthony Roseto, DBA EMM Holdings, Inc., unless otherwise noted. All rights reserved. No part of this publication
may be reproduced in any form or by any means, except short exerpts for review, without the prior written permission of the
publisher. All names, characters, events, and locales in this publication are entirely fictional. Any similarity to actual persons,
living or dead, events, or places, without satiric intent is coincidental.
Monarch Comics is on the web at www.monarchcomics.com

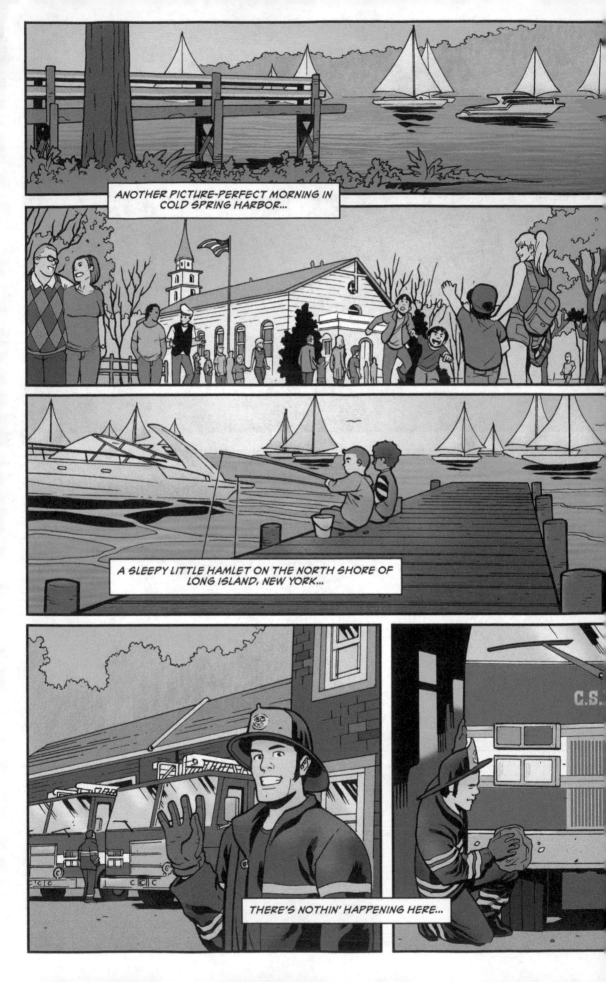

IN FACT, NOTHING EVER HAPPENS AROUND HERE...

AND THAT'S THE WAY FOLKS LIKE IT...

PEACEFUL...

QUIET...

SERENE...

WHY ARE YOU ATTACKING ME?

ACTUALLY I DON'T RIGHTLY *KNOW*.

WHAT... I MEAN, *WHO*, ARE YOU?

I'M *MIKE*... AND...

I DON'T REALLY KNOW WHAT I AM...

OH...

I *BARELY* REMEMBER WHAT CAME BEFORE THIS MOMENT.

I WAS *TRYING* TO FIGURE IT OUT, BUT EVERYONE WAS AFTER ME.

OK...UM, *MIKE*...

LET'S GET YOU INSIDE AND SEE WHAT WE CAN FIGURE OUT.

RUDGE, WHAT'S GOING ON HERE? DO WE HAVE THE BEAST? DO WE HAVE A PERIMETER? DO WE HAVE A *CLUE*?

WE'RE WORKING ON IT, MA'AM.

ARE WE?

SYNE, WHAT DO *YOU* HAVE FOR ME?

SECURITY VIDEO.

GET YOUR ACT TOGETHER, RUDGE. TAKE A CLUE FROM YOUR BUDDY.

YES, MA'AM.

STOP CALLING ME *MA'AM*, RUDGE.

ANYTHING ON THE VIDEO?

I THINK WE GOT *HIM*.

REALLY? *HIM*?! SHOW ME.

CHEE-OH.

)CLICK(

WHAT?!?

WHAT HAS
HAPPENED?

WHERE AM I?

WHERE IS
MY..?

OH MY!

MANNY!
BEHIND YOU!

SHAI-POO?

OKAY MIKE, TURN IT *DOWN* A NOTCH. *KILLING* THIS TALKING HEAD WON'T HELP.

I AM SORRY, MICHAEL. MY WORK INVOLVED TRANSPORTATION, NOT TRANSMUTATION.

YOU AND THE BABOON SHOULD HAVE SIMPLY *SWITCHED* PLACES. YOU SHOULD NOT HAVE BEEN *COMBINED!* WE CAN *FIX* THIS!

WE?! WHAT *WE?!* YOU SAID *YOU!* YOU SAID *YOU* CAN FIX THIS!

CAN YOU!?!

I BELIEVE I CAN. BUT WE, MANNY AND MYSELF, THAT IS, WILL NEED YOUR HELP.

HELP DOING *WHAT?*

WELL, FIRST OFF, WE MUST GET OUT OF HERE...

SO, DOC, YOU KNOW WHERE THIS CAMP HERO PLACE IS?

ROGER THAT. EVERYONE OUT HERE KNOWS THAT PLACE.

IS *THAT* YOUR CAMPER?

YEAH, I KNOW, IT'S NOT MUCH.

YOU *KIDDIN'*? LOOKS *WONDERFUL*! NICE AN' SPACIOUS!

¡AY!

9-1-1, WHAT IS YOUR EMERGENCY?

GRAN MONO QUE HABLA!

WE GOT SOMETHING. OUT IN MONTAUK.

WHAT IS IT?

MOTEL STAFF HAS EYES ON OUR MONKEY-MAN.

ALL RIGHT, THEN. PACK THIS UP. WE'RE MOVING EAST.

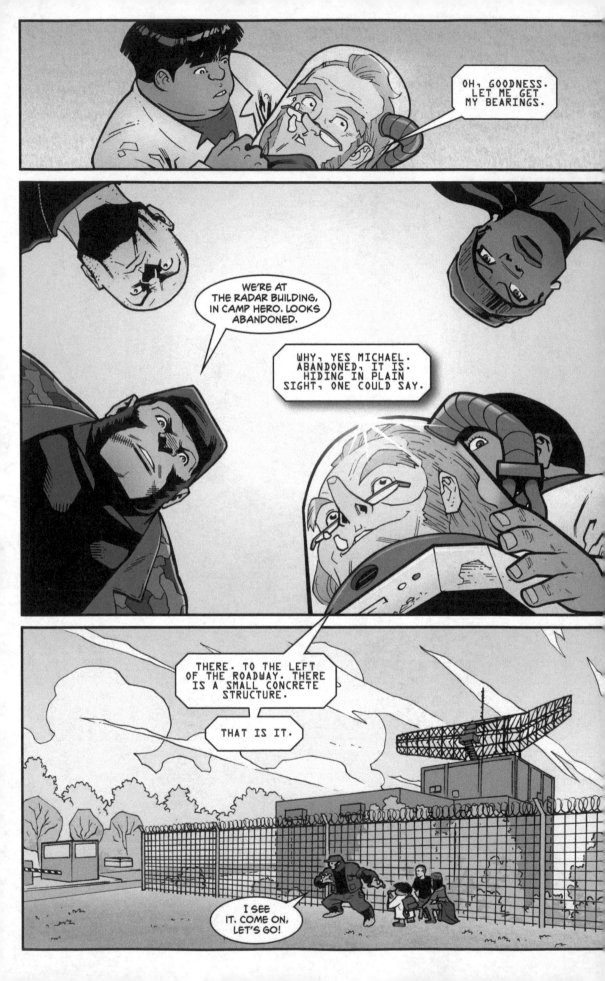

HUUMMMZRKTUMMMM

THE OBJECTS WE SEEK ARE OVER IN THIS DIRECTION, IF YOU WOULD, PLEASE.

OK, MOONPIE, YOU HAVE A WAY TO FIX ME HERE, RIGHT?

WELL, NO. NOT PRECISELY, MICHAEL.

HUUMMMZRKTUMMMM

WHAT?!?

I NEVER INDICATED THAT I WOULD BE ABLE TO REVERSE YOUR, ER, PROBLEM HERE...

HUUMMMMZRKTUMMMMM

WHAT IS THAT HUMMING!?!

HEY, I HEAR SOMETHING TOO.

YEAH.

YES, MANNY. LET US ACQUIRE THAT WHICH WE CAME FOR.

WE CAME HERE FOR A FUNNY HAT?

THIS FUNNY HAT, MICHAEL, IS OUR FIRST STEP TOWARD YOUR RESTORATION.

AND THE PAPYRUS, MANNY.

SHAI-POO.

WHAT'S THAT?

THAT, LINA, THAT IS HOW WE GET TO THE SECOND STEP OF MICHAEL'S RESTORATION.

SEVERAL HOURS LATER AND MANY MILES WEST...

...ENTERING THE BIG APPLE.

EUREKA! I THINK I'VE GOT IT!

CHARLESTON! WE MUST TRAVEL TO CHARLESTON, SOUTH CAROLINA!

HUH?

SEE HERE NOW, MICHAEL, IT'S A RIDDLE.

SAY WHAT NOW?

IT'S IN AN ANCIENT DIALECT, THE CODE OF ANGELS.

REALLY?

IT SAYS, "TO GAIN WISDOM, ONE MUST FOLLOW THE OX TO THE TAVERN..."

"...IN THE CITY THAT GUARDS HER TEMPLES, CUSTOMS, AND LAW."

RIGHT, OF COURSE IT DOES, AND THAT MEANS ...CHARLESTON?

PEESTA.

THEY KNOW MY *NAME!* THEY HAVE MY *CAR!*

CALM *DOWN!* THEY HAVE NO REAL LEADS. THAT'S WHY THEY'RE USING THE MEDIA.

OOH! SHRIMPS!

SHAI-*POO!*

YOU GUYS FIGURE OUT WHERE THIS TAVERN IS?

I FEEL THAT OUR BEST BET WILL BE THE TAVERN AT RAINBOW ROW. IT HAS BEEN THERE SINCE THE 17TH CENTURY.

YEAH, WHAT HE SAID.

THE FEDS KNOW WHO I AM, DOC. THEY PUT ME ON THE TV.

THAT PICTURE DIDN'T EVEN LOOK LIKE YOU.

OH, YEAH, WELL, THAT'S *REAL* COMFORTING.

THE STORY BEHIND THE SONG BEHIND THE STORY

The Origin of Evil Monkey Man by Blake

(Yes, it truly is based on a song.)

A lot of my friends in high school were in bands. They would play school events as well as the occasional gig in one of the all-ages clubs around the island (*that's Long Island, New York.*) Live music was a big thing back then, in the late 1980's. One of those bands was **FL!NG Lo!S**, in which my buddy, Frank, was chief songwriter, bassist, and singer. One of their songs was "Evil Monkey Man." It was, is, a catchy pop-metal screamer with a neat sci-fi theme and showcased guitarist Anthony's six-string acrobatics. In short, I liked that song. Quite a bit. With just a few verses, Frank outlined an outlandish cartoon-like story featuring a small cast of really intriguing characters. It was just a sketch, maybe, but the song, and its main protagonist, the Monkey Man, made an impression, and stuck with me for years.

Later, in the early 1990's, I was inking backgrounds for another dear friend, the late Mike Esposito. As we drove back and forth to drop off and pick up pages at the publishers, we were plotting a new venture with which to enter and conquer the vibrant comic business of the day. Eventually, Mike convinced his long-time friend and collaborator, the late Ross Andru, to join our project. Ross' contribution would be his creation, **The Strobe Warrior**. While Mike and I logged innumerable miles transporting artwork and developing our business plan, we also tended to listen to music. Mike would school this youngster on the history and virtuosity of Frank Sinatra and his band, while I would share my favorite bands with him at full volume. What was amazing about this cross-generation music germination experiment was that it really worked - one minute Mike would be driving down the L.I.E. tapping along to Rush or Metallica, moments later we'd be belting out the standards with the Chairman of the Board. To put things in perspective, at the time, I was in my early twenties, Mike was in his late sixties.

During the comics craze of the 90's, a lot of publishers started using all sorts of gimmicks and publishing all sorts of special editions. Of course, we planned to do the same with our comics. As our business solidified and money was being raised, I started designing the "Special Limited Edition" release for *Strobe Warrior*, which, we decided, would include a CD of music. What music? Well, I asked Frank and **FL!NG Lo!S** to come up with a song for *Strobe Warrior.* And they did. Unfortunately, all of our planning was for naught, and the whole thing fell apart. I continued working with Mike for a while, mostly on recreations of works from his legendary years at Marvel and DC, but we eventually drifted apart and I went to work in the recording industry. Ross had passed unexpectedly in 1993, and Mike passed in 2010. Andru and Esposito were inducted into the Will Eisner Comic Book Hall of Fame in 2007.

That could have been the end of the story. But in 2014 Frank called me to say he wanted to release "The Strobe Warrior" song and asked me to design a cover. Being now in the age of Facebook, I looked up one of my pals from SVA (The School of Visual Arts,) Hunter McFalls, and asked him to do the cover with me. I think it actually came out pretty cool.

And that could have been the end of the story. But Hunter was drawing a comic called *Witch Hunter*, and he and the writer/publisher, Vincent Ferrante, needed a colorist for their book. Since I had just colored the cover for "Strobe Warrior," Hunter called me and asked, "Hey Blake, do you color comics?" I answered, "No, not really" Hunter continued, "Do you want to color comics?" I again replied, "No, not really." Now, I don't know what was lost in translation, but somehow Hunter heard "yes." So he sent me a pinup to try-out on. I actually had to watch a video on YouTube just to figure out how to color the thing. Anyway, they hired me, and I started coloring *Witch Hunter.*

Fast forward a couple months, and I had reason to be in New York. (I did and currently reside in Virginia.) So I proposed a visit with Vincent and met with him, along with another SVA buddy, Phil Avelli, at Vin's place in Connecticut, with Hunter video-conferencing in. During the meeting, Vin announced his intention to expand his publishing roster and asked if any of us had any ideas. Of course, Phil and Hunter had a bunch. When it was my turn to answer, I kinda glanced sheepishly around and said "Evil Monkey Man?" as more of a question than a statement. Vin said something to the effect of "Great, let's do it!" And that was that. I left the meet and greet thinking, "What the heck did I just get myself into?"

It wasn't the first time I'd thought about adapting Frank's song into a comic. As Ross, Mike and I were developing *Strobe Warrior,* and I was asking Frank to write that song, I was also jotting notes in my sketchbook about maybe translating Frank's "Evil Monkey Man" song into a comic book. I noted then that my preferred artist was to be Stan Goldberg, who was pencilling most of the Archie stuff Mike was inking at the time. Years later, I even found a little doodle of a monkey on the back of some Archie art that Mike had likely sketched while he and I were sitting around his kitchen table. So, for the 2016 New York Comic Com, I simply adapted Frank's lyrics and released the following five-page one-shot illustrated by Angelo Ty "Bong" Dazo. Unfortunately, Bong also passed, in 2018. All five pages of his amazing *Evil Monkey Man!* art are presented here for the first time since 2016. Enjoy.

THE EVOLUTION OF EVIL MONKEY MAN

In the beginning...

While I was working on the original 2016 NYCC preview my daughter was also starting her art career...here's *The Saga of Evil Monkey Man* #1 Variant Cover by *Meaghan Seals.* This image, as well as her likeness, feature prominently in issue #1 as she actually names Mike as "an evil monkey man" to reporters.

Dr. Monke Moon.

Early concept sketches by *Russ Braun* (*The Boys,* Disney, Marvel, DC)

2016 preview cover pencil sketch by *Bong Dazo* (*Avengers, Deadpool, Star Wars*) and on the opposite page, his finished cover illustration...

Although Bong's artwork was stunning and well-received at NYCC, as I started to flesh out my ideas for the saga, I realized I intended to go in a different direction visually. With fond memories of binge-watching *Scooby-Doo, Where Are You!* influencing my mindset, I went in search of an artist with a different style...

Episode One pencils by **Butch Mapa** (Zenecope, Top Shelf, Image, Marvel/IDW)

If Bong and I had continued, this likely would have been the cover for Episode One...

So, after viewing probably a hundred portfolios, I chose another wonderful Filipino artist, Butch Mapa.
Together we have now finished the first of three "seasons," or four "episodes," of *The Saga of Evil Monkey Man!*
Here are some examples of Butch's great design work, followed by a gallery of his covers for the series.

COVER GALLERY · EPISODE ONE
DESIGN BY BLAKE · ART BY BUTCH MAPA & K MICHAEL RUSSELL
HOMAGE TO THE GREAT SCI-FI & HORROR MOVIE POSTERS OF THE 1950's ESPECIALLY
"FORBIDDEN PLANET" (1956) & "CREATURE FROM THE BLACK LAGOON" (1954)

COVER GALLERY · EPISODE TWO
DESIGN BY BLAKE · ART BY BUTCH MAPA & K MICHAEL RUSSELL
HOMAGE AND PLAY ON THE SCENE FROM "FRANKENSTEIN" (1931) WHEN THE MONSTER
COMES OUT OF THE WOODS TO FIND LITTLE MARIA PICKING DAISIES LAKESIDE.

COVER GALLERY · EPISODE THREE
DESIGN BY BLAKE · ART BY BUTCH MAPA & K MICHAEL RUSSELL
HOMAGE TO THE BRILLIANT "MONSTERS INC." (2001)
MOVIE POSTER AND VIDEO COVER FROM DISNEY/PIXAR.

COVER GALLERY · EPISODE FOUR
DESIGN BY BLAKE · ART BY BUTCH MAPA & K MICHAEL RUSSELL
HOMAGE TO THE KING, JACK KIRBY.

CPSIA information can be obtained
at www.ICGtesting.com
Printed in the USA
LVHW021508080421
683869LV00008B/449